Pe
Gets a Job

written by Feana Tu'akoi
illustrated by Rieko Woodford-Robinson

KAEDEN ❤ BOOKS™

Peacock was bored.

"There's nothing to do," he said.
"I just prance around the farm all day."

"You need a job," said Rooster. "Then you'd have lots to do."

"Yes!" said Peacock. "I'll get a job here on the farm."

Peacock tried to chase the mice.
"Stop!" said Cat. "That's my job!"

Peacock tried to lay the eggs.

"Stop!" said Hen. "That's my job!"

Peacock tried to eat the scraps.
"Stop!" said Pig. "That's my job!"

Peacock tried to catch the flies.

"Stop!" said Spider. "That's my job!"

Peacock tried to make the milk.
"Stop!" said Cow. "That's my job!"

Peacock tried to herd the sheep.

"Stop!" said Dog. "That's my job!"

Peacock tried to pull the wagon.

"Stop!" said Horse. "That's my job!"

"It's not fair!" said Peacock. "Everyone has a job, except me."

He pranced around the farm and frowned.

Some visitors came to the farm. Peacock crowed loudly and pranced around in front of them. Then he spread out his tail so they could admire him.

"This is fun!" said Peacock. "I like this job!"

Finally, Peacock had a job on the farm too.